WOLF'S COMING!

For Michael and James

No part of this publication may be reproduced, stored
in a retrieval system, or transmitted in any form or by
any means, electronic, mechanical, photocopying, recording,
or otherwise, without written permission of the publisher.
For information regarding permission, write to
Carolrhoda Books, Inc., a division of Lerner Publishing Group,
241 First Avenue North, Minneapolis, MN 55401.

ISBN: 978-0-545-23846-5

12 11 10 9 8 7 6 5 4 3   10 11 12 13 14 15/0

Printed in the U.S.A.   08

First Scholastic printing, January 2010

WOLF'S COMING!

JOE KULKA

SCHOLASTIC INC.
New York Toronto London Auckland
Sydney Mexico City New Delhi Hong Kong

A distant howl rides the breeze,
echoing through all the trees.

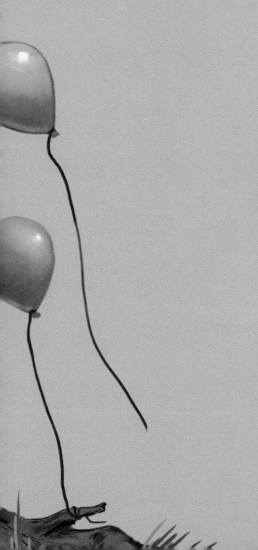

Hurry, HURRY!
Don't be slow!
Follow me.
C'mon, let's go!

A shadowy figure climbs the hill,
getting **close** and **closer** still.

Faster, FASTER!
Take my hand!
Run back home
like we planned.

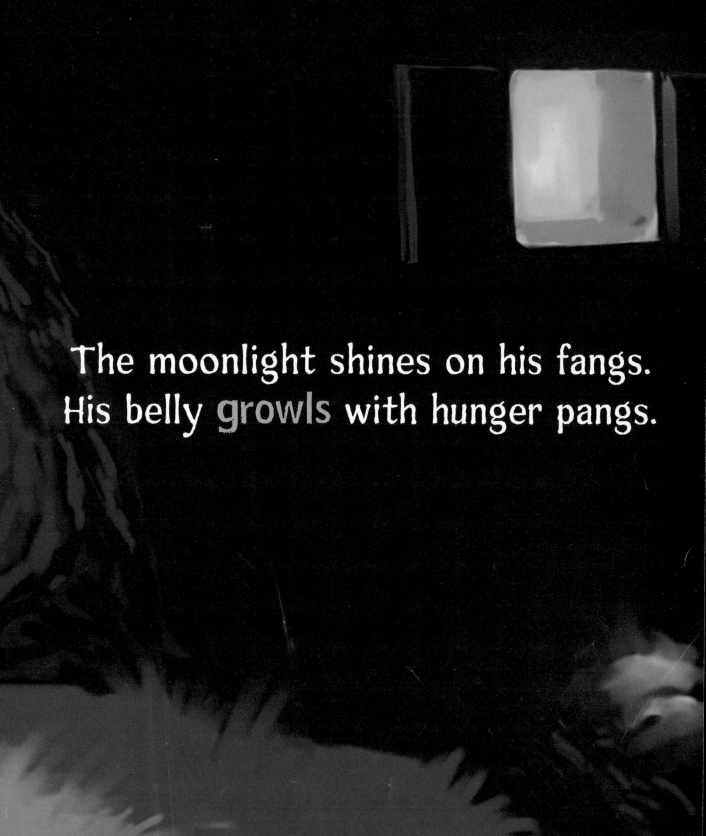

The moonlight shines on his fangs.
His belly growls with hunger pangs.

Closer, CLOSER.
Next to me.
Pull the shade
so he can't see.

WOLF'S COMING!

Glowing ember eyes appear.
Pointed ears strain to hear.

Hush now, HUSH NOW.
Not a peep.
You must be still,
like you're asleep.

WOLF'S HERE!

The front door opens with a creak.
The big wolf leans in for a peek.

Tightly, TIGHTLY,
shut your eyes.
With all your might yell . . .

SUR

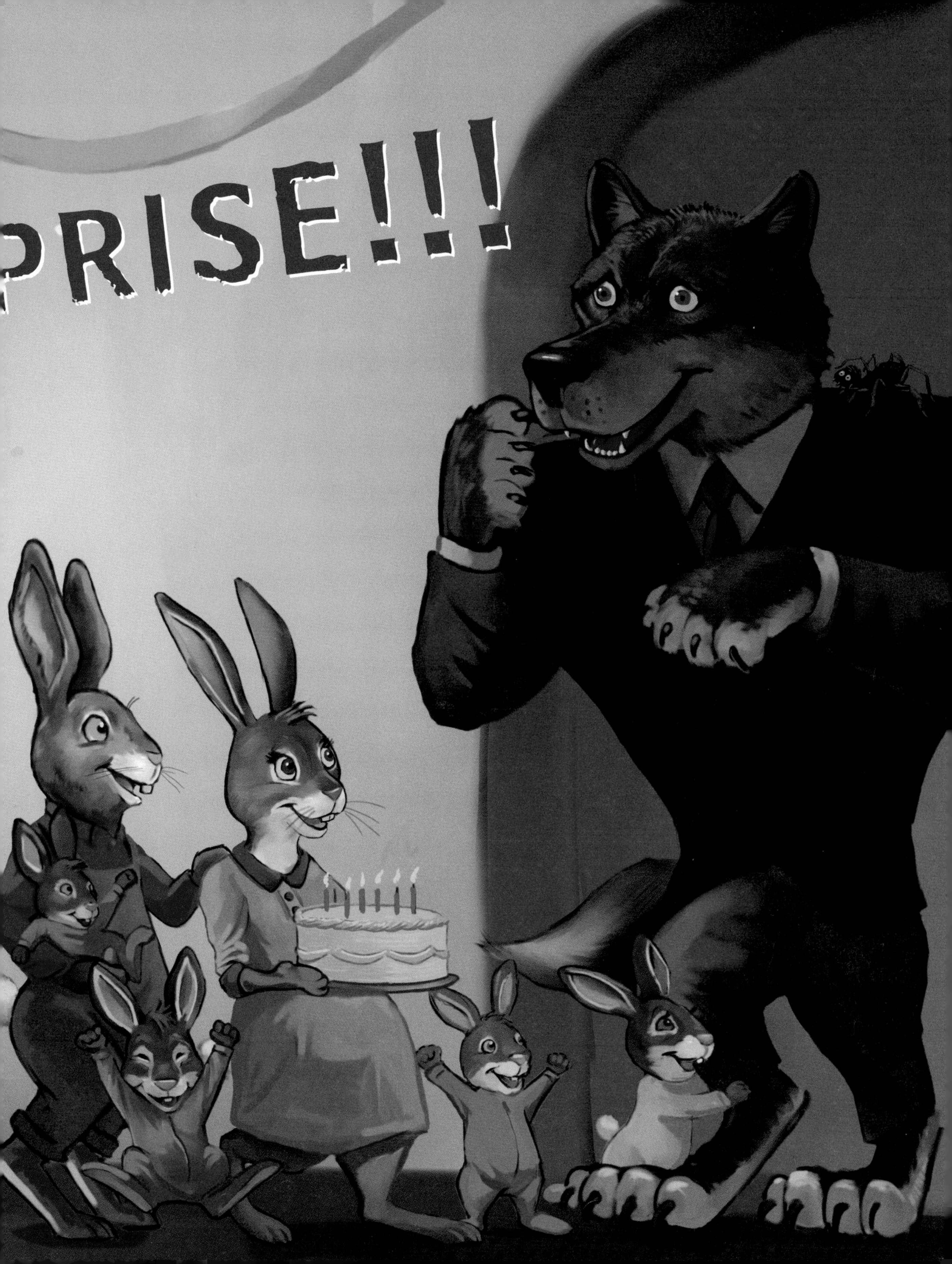
PRISE!!!

Laughing, LAUGHING!
So much fun!
Cake and pizza for everyone!

HAPPY BIRTHDAY, WOLF!